THE WITCH'S GOODBYE

THE OKRITH NOVELLAS
BOOK FIVE

A.K. MULFORD

Paperback 978-1-923184-10-7

Ebook 978-1-923184-09-1

Cover by MiblArt

Map by Holly Dunn Designs

Interior Formatting by K. Elle Morrison

CONTENT WARNING

This book contains themes of violence, loss, grief, fire, suicidal ideation, as well as sexually explicit scenes.

Spoiler Warning

This story contains mild spoilers from The High Mountain Court!

NORTHERN COU[RT]
Murreneir
Brufdoran
DRUNEHAN
Vurstyn
HIGH MOUNTAIN COURT
Valtene
YEXSHIRE
SWIFTHILL
WESTERN COURT
SEA OF CALLIPHO
Silver Sands Harbor
OKRITH

N
SEA OF WETAMUIR
enport
Falhampton
ROTTED PEAK
EASTERN COURT
WYNREACH
Haarsmouth
SOUTHERN COURT
Crushwold
SAXBRIDGE

CHAPTER ONE

The raucous music was so loud, she had to cup her hand around her ear to hear Lord Bracken's story. Despite missing every other word, Carys laughed at the appropriate times, conducted by the facial expressions of the others around her. Wine filled her veins with a pleasant buzz. The hours of the day had been eaten up in the Spring Equinox festivities and she'd been halfway to being drunk since mid-morning.

The guests had arrived with the dawn, all gathering to drink and celebrate the end of the winter months. The entire bottom floor of Hilgaard was bedecked with garlands, fresh herbs, and ornate table settings. The last of the winter fare was brought out in a sumptuous buffet, and many a conversation was about the fruits soon to be blossoming from the trees. Of course, in the Southern Court, the food was bountiful year-round, but the sweetest scented time of year was still the spring when the trees bloomed every shade from lavender to fuchsia to iridescent yellow.

Her father, Lord Hilgaard, threw these lavish parties that were attended by all the fae Lords in the region, some even traveling as far as the Northern Court with their families, much to the Southern Court Queen's chagrin. Since the Battle of Yexshire, the diplomacy between the North and South was very much strained, but Lord Hilgaard was determined to ignore everything that was happening beyond his castle gates, especially on the Solstice. He enjoyed the praise and accolades too much before. Now, it was only to keep up appearances.

The Summer Solstice was the Queen's and the Queen's alone, but the spring had much more options for entertaining. Many of the fae royals and courtiers liked to flock to the Southern Court for the winter months, where the weather was still balmy and the snow was a distant thought. The spring was still frost-bitten and gray in the North, whereas the Southern Court was blooming with life and color, especially in the jungles surrounding Hilgaard castle.

The castle sat perfectly nestled between two jungle-clad hills, halfway between Arboa and Saxbridge. Dwarfed only by a giant amasa tree, the castle rose up through the canopy, its spires piercing into the clouds. The home was prestigious with stained-glass windows and stately sharp architecture in the Northern stylings, but warm too, with coral roses rambling up the hedges and a tinkling fountain by the gate to welcome weary travelers. Lord Hilgaard took it as a personal offense if nobility didn't stop along their travels between the two larger cities. Of course, Lord Hilgaard didn't have much of an opinion on anything anymore.

"Where is his Lordship?" Lady Crisilla Vanalton asked, the older fae Lady sauntering through the crowd, butting people out of the way with her ample hips. Her shrill voice cut easily through the clamor as she came into view.

Carys put on her practiced air of indifference, tinged with a mild displeasure that she'd learned from these high society ministrations. She knew how to look down her nose at everyone, even those a head taller than herself.

"He is giving a tour of his new gallery acquisitions," she said. "Did he not invite you along?" She gave the fae matron a pitying glare, pouting her lips, and making her surrounding friends cackle with venom-tipped delight.

Otho Denton laughed so hard his wine spilled over his goblet and splashed onto the intricately embroidered carpet. No one seemed to notice besides Carys though. Lords were excused for acting without decorum in the way the Ladies were not.

Oh well, Carys thought with glee, *time to commission a new rug.*

Lady Vanalton wasn't cowed by Carys's rebuke though. She narrowed her piercing pale blue eyes at Carys, her mouth pinched. The second cousin of King Vostemur, Lady Vanalton had probably seen her fair share of horrors and knew how to navigate through this pit of snakes just as well as Carys, probably even more so.

"Come to think of it," Lady Vanalton demurred, cooling herself with her tasteless peacock feather fan. "I haven't seen Lord Hilgaard at any of his celebrations in some time."

Carys was already raking through her arsenal of witty retorts, her fair-weathered friends clinging to her every movement, waiting for her to say something vicious. The raven-haired twins, Basina and Gabrielle, clasped each other's hands and leaned in, enraptured, but a voice cut Carys off before she had a chance to speak.

"Ah, there's my Fated," a smooth baritone sounded behind her, and a moment later, she was engulfed in the smell of snowflowers and Arboan sun-baked clay.

"Lady Vanalton," Sy addressed the matron with a bob of his chin, his midnight eyes cold and condescending. His lanky body seemed to grow another inch from sheer force of will alone. There'd been a time not too long ago when he and Carys had been the same height. Now, he was a whole head taller than her and his lean body was still catching up to its newfound size.

"Lord Almah," Crisilla replied just as icily, but she offered a half-bow regardless. Offending someone's Fated in front of them was just asking for a knife to the guts . . . or, in high society, to be assigned a seat closest to the stench of the stables at dinner and the last cut of roast.

"If you'll excuse me, I need to speak to my Fated in private," Sy said. He gave her a haughty wink, his eyes telling Crisilla exactly what he was planning on doing with his Fated. Her lips curled with distaste as Sy's hand landed on the small of Carys's back and he bent to brush a kiss to her temple. It made Carys's skin bloom with heat every time he touched her.

The word rolled so easily off his tongue. *Fated.*

He said it so proudly as he threaded his fingers through Carys's own and yanked her to a stand. His hands circled her waist and he kissed her deeply, his tongue plundering her mouth as Carys's friends tittered. Of all her friends, Carys was the only one who had a Fated. She knew of others who were destined by the Fates to have someone, but none of them had been found or actualized. The blue witches were capricious with their visions.

Carys puffed up her chest a little, smug that she was special in this way. She'd lived with Sy in Arboa for most of the year, but was called back by her father out of necessity. Her father had protested her Fated moving in with them during the last few months. They were still so young and yet to be married, he'd complained, but if the Gods ordained it, then it was a losing battle. Besides, he loved Sy like a son . . . and he didn't have any fight in him anymore anyway.

Carys flitted through the crowd, smirking and simpering at the throng of guests adorned in their fae finery. Her father would be so proud if he could see this grand display. Carys threw renowned parties lavish enough they would impress all but the Queen of Saxbridge herself . . . maybe it was time to start a menagerie?

Sy dragged Carys out into the coolness of the hall, the raucous sounds blissfully dampening. He hauled her up another flight of curving stone steps, and out onto the second-floor balcony before he spoke. Carys couldn't tell if his urgency was driven by lust or bad news—they seemed to have both in equal measure of late.

"Is he okay?" Carys asked as Sy shut the door behind her.

"He's awake," Sy replied, already knowing who "he" was. "He's asking for you."

"Probably with more of his stories for me. Do all fae Lords need a ten tome biography of their life?" Carys rolled her eyes. "As if anyone would read it. Or he'll have even more directions for the household under my care. No one will know I'm using the summer cutlery with the autumnal linens when he's gone anyway." Carys grabbed a handful of Sy's pewter jacket and tugged him to her. "He can wait."

She lifted on her toes to kiss him, relishing the feeling of her lips on his own—warm, soft, so all-encompassing that she could forget about all the roiling emotions deep within her.

But Sy pulled back. "The healers want to give him more brew and put him back under."

Carys ignored that statement and instead licked the seam of Sy's mouth, imploring him to kiss her back. This frenzy—*this* is what they did best. Sy relented for a minute, his hands sliding around Carys's waist and yanking her against him. His tongue dipped into her mouth and he tasted her, his hands roving her curves for one indulgent moment before he let out a frustrated groan and dropped his forehead to hers. Carys's hand slid down his torso, heading straight toward his trousers when Sy took a whole step back from her.

"I think you should go speak to him," he said tightly, letting out the slow sigh that Carys knew was the sound of him trying to cool his libido. Oh, how she loved to taunt him. "Who knows how many times you have left," Sy added. "I know how much this means to you."

Well, if anything could douse ice on her desire, it would be that sentiment. *How much he means to you.* Sy had no clue. He thought Carys looked at her father like he'd hung the moon in the sky, but she was just exceptionally good at hiding her contempt.

Carys balled her hands into fists, clenching her jaw so tightly she thought she might crack a tooth. "Get out of my way, then," she said, shoving Sy aside and storming back into the castle.

CHAPTER TWO

arys paced down the hall, a bitter scowl on her face, then she thought better of it and schooled her expression into a steely neutral. Her father told her the expression would give her premature wrinkles and that she didn't want to look like a haggard old crone. *This advice coming from a fae who had lines deep enough she was pretty sure she could slot a coin into them and they would hold.*

The music of the party below mocked her as she climbed up and up and up. Her father's bed chamber had been moved to the tower where no servants or guests might accidentally stumble across him, the stairs too steep and winding for him to descend anymore.

Two brown witches huddled in front of the last stairwell whispering to each other. Their bronze-tinted magic sputtered lifeless from their fingertips as if their magic had been all but drained from their efforts. Their fatigued faces said everything: it wouldn't be long now.

It was uncommon, to say the least, for fae to die of mysterious ailments. But these brown witches hadn't found a single reason why her father's health would continue to dwindle. They whispered of curses behind his back, but who would curse such an esteemed Lord?

Carys had brought in witches from far and wide to see him, paying them handsomely to keep his secrets. But acquiring good help was difficult since King Vostemur put a bounty on red witch heads and all witches were being hunted in return. Convincing a witch to make the journey from the Western Court—even with the promise of mountains of gold—was a tall order these days. The pass through Silver Sands was still rife with witch hunters.

Carys had spent months planning how she would tell people her father had died. An accident perhaps? He fell off his horse or on his sword? She could throw his body in the Crushwold River and say he drowned . . . Of course, that would involve carting his body through the jungle, and the thought of that turned her stomach. Sy would do it for her, she knew he would, but still, there had to be a better way.

She hated that her flicker of hope had morphed into bitter defeat. That she was planning how to explain his death even while he still lived. Some days she thought it might be kinder just to end him herself. She didn't see him coming back from this mysterious malady, but she also couldn't linger in this liminal state, unable to save him or grieve him. He was the very last of her family and, even though she resented him to her very core, she couldn't bear the thought of being the only Hilgaard left either.

She'd already paid off the remainder of her household staff and instructed them that, when the time came, to seek employ in Saxbridge or journey with her to Arboa. Gods, she missed Arboa. She missed the salty brine of the ocean and the scent of snowflowers that wafted up to the manor on the hill. She missed the food and the songs and the people most of all.

It felt wrong to be waiting *hopefully* for her father to die. She thought she'd escaped him by moving to Arboa with Sy, but then he had to go and fall ill and drag her into this life again—this haunted castle in the middle of the woods. The house, though beautiful, had been a constant reminder of her mother's untimely death, and the halls had been filled with a heavy cloud for all of her youth. She felt the darkness that must have infected her mother's mind as keenly as if it were her own.

"Move," Carys gritted out to the whispering witches. They scattered like mice as she shouldered her way between them and up the steps. "Useless."

What good was a brown witch who couldn't do their fucking job?

The last thing she wanted was another progress report from them either. She didn't want them to spin some dire prognosis into something gentler. She just wanted to know what he wanted now so she could find another glass of wine and get on with this party—*his legacy*—pretenses she could soon drop in favor of the mourning daughter and eventually know some peace. Once her duty was done, she could return to Arboa and lose herself in its tropical waters and the body of her Fated.

Carys pushed open the creaking tower door, the smell of rot accosting her senses. Even with the heady floral scent of brew clinging to the curtains and lingering in the air, the space smelled like death. The circular room was dimly lit with only a few bedside candles lighting the expanse.

"Carys," her father rasped, and with that, her steely facade fractured an inch. He was once stoic, proud. This weak and pleading voice wasn't that of someone she knew at all. And curse all the Gods, she still loved him, even if she resented him too. If only her feelings could be singular. Life would be so much easier.

"Father," she said, swallowing the emotions constricting her throat.

She wandered over to his bed, too big for the room, and perched on his rumpled bed sheets. His hands were gnarled, the skin pink and peeling, his face so filled with decay the only part of him she still recognized were those brilliant blue eyes—her eyes. His sickness had taken him so fast, she still couldn't comprehend the father she knew and loved was gone.

"The party is going swimmingly," she said when her father didn't immediately volunteer any more words. "You should see the Allstads. They practically had smoke coming from their ears with jealousy."

His thin lips pulled to one side at that. He would've loved it, making others jealous, upholding the Hilgaard name. Her father always had a tinge of greatness, loftier ambitions than a fine castle in the middle of the forest, and Carys was the conduit with which he would attain them—Fated to the Lord of Arboa, distant relation to King Vostemur, best friend to the Heir of Saxbridge.

She picked up a discarded cloth from his bedside and dipped it in the bowl of water beside it. She blotted his forehead, performing an act of tenderness she couldn't quite bring herself to feel. Her father lifted his curled hand, swatting it away. He would've hated others to see him like this. He'd made Carys vow a hundred times to never allow anyone to learn what had become of him. Too vain. Sy and Carys were the only fae allowed to visit him, all of his past comrades and acquaintances pushed away with excuses and lies.

"What is it you wished to speak to me about?" Carys finally prompted, feeling uncomfortable sitting in the quiet and just listening to his belabored breathing.

"I won't make it through another night," he said, taking long gasping breaths between each word. "I don't *want* to make it through another night." His voice was so watery and weak, she knew he spoke true.

Carys mindlessly adjusted her many jewel-studded necklaces and toyed with the golden ring around her thumb, hoping one day her fingers would be plump enough to move it to a more meaningful digit. Her father noted the action and touched the ring with his thumb.

"Your mother's ring," he said fondly, a hint of melancholy threading his words that he had hidden better when he was well. "She used to wear it on a necklace, her fingers too big when she was pregnant with you."

Carys couldn't remember her mother at all, but she missed her nonetheless. The staff at the palace had tried to keep her memory alive as best they could, but it didn't really make a difference.

"It doesn't really go with that dress," her father added. "A gold ring against silver lace?"

Ah. There he was. Carys hastily removed her mother's ring. Her cheeks and ears burned as she tucked it into the lining of her gown. She straightened her shoulders and rose from the bed.

"Rest well, Father," she said.

"Carys, wait," her father implored, and she paused, glancing at his gaunt face from over her shoulder.

Maybe this was it. Maybe it was time for them to truly have a heart-to-heart. Maybe on the precipice of death he'd finally embrace her for all she was. For the briefest moment, she permitted herself to dream of his next words: I love you, I'm proud of you, *you are enough.*

But instead he said, "Can you send Sy in? I need to talk to him."

CHAPTER THREE

The jungle beyond was awash with evening color, tropical birds nestling in trees for the night, and monkeys howling across the canopies. Carys rested her elbows on the balustrade and breathed in the balmy forest air. Her eyes kept misting of their own volition and she wasn't really sure why. She watched the line of carriages disappearing down the shadowed roads in either direction—most to Saxbridge and some back to Arboa. Carys was meant to host a few stragglers that evening but decided it was better to send them all away. If her father was truly going to die that night, then she didn't need any other people bearing witness to whatever excuse she devised for his death.

She let out another ragged sigh, telling herself it was normal to mourn her father's death. But the feeling inside her wasn't just that. It was so much more. Soon he'd be gone, and then what? Just move back to Arboa and use the castle as a holiday home? Go from being one Lord's daughter to another Lord's wife? Would this dark little shadow follow along over her head forever? Would this emptiness always exist within her?

The sky faded from burnt orange to a purpling bruise on the horizon. How did she get here? How was this the person she'd become? It felt like she blinked and went from being a girl with ribbons in her hair to the head of her family—the only one propping up the illustrious Hilgaard name. She felt her whole childhood being dragged in the undertow of the person she *should* be —the person she now *was* through shame and example and fear of her father's disapproval. But now that he wasn't here to disapprove, who would she be now? Would she just look to Sy to tell her how to feel about herself? Was that what her mother had done?

As if summoned by her own thoughts, the door to the balcony opened and a confident set of footsteps echoed out.

"What did he say?" she asked without turning.

Sy's hands slid around her waist, his lean chest pressing to her back and filling her with heat. She loved the way his hands possessively roved her body, the ownership in his hold. It kept all her dizzying thoughts at bay. So what if her father was dying? At least she'd still have someone to keep her from the loneliness that had plagued her all of her childhood. Sy was a guarantee, a Fates-ordained constant, and for that she was grateful.

"He said nothing of importance," Sy murmured as his hands skimmed higher and he palmed her breasts over the thin material of her dress. "More of his frippery."

He pinched her nipples, eliciting a moan. Her head fell back onto his shoulder and her eyelids fluttered closed. The welcome pleasure pushed some of her tangled thoughts to the background. She pressed her ass back into his already hardening length. They always seemed so ready for each other, always right on the knife's edge of desire.

Carys thanked the Gods for their mating bond, that her lust could supersede everything else. Her desire for Sy was like its own kind of drug: more potent than wine or brew, it dulled her senses to everything but him, and Gods, did she want to feel numb.

As Carys moved to spin around, Sy grabbed her by the hips and propped her on the balcony. Her ass hung over the side as her hands threaded through his dark hair. She stole a glance down to the drop, only a couple feet with the stable roof right below them. She'd used this route many nights to sneak out to Arboa when her father told her she was too young to visit Sy.

"I'm not going to drop you." Sy let out a rough chuckle. He grabbed her chin and pulled her face back to his. "Tonight was masterful, my love."

He kissed her so thoroughly, so completely, that the rest of the world faded away. She melted into that kiss, her mouth opening for his tongue, a groan rumbling up his throat. She hooked her ankles around his tapered hips and pulled him flush against her, clinging to him.

As she ground wantonly against his erection, the friction through their lightweight clothing made her core pulse. Sy grabbed fistfuls of her delicate lace dress and carelessly yanked it up, the sound of ripping fabric filling the twilight.

Carys frantically grabbed for his belt buckle, freeing his cock and positioning him at her entrance. Her core was already slick, her thighs damp. He slammed into her, already knowing from her hitched breaths how ready she was. She moaned against his lips, rocking her hips to get him to hit that spot that made her eyes roll back. She could tell by the way his fingers clawed at her back and the feral groans that he wouldn't last long.

Sy tried to hold off until Carys had tipped over that edge, but ultimately couldn't, not with the way she rode him, chasing her own release. When he stilled with a barked groan, spilling into her, she reached down and rubbed herself, circling with wanton abandon until her muscles were fluttering around him and her chest was exploding with a white-hot orgasm.

They fucked in a selfish, ravenous way—taking the pleasure they so desperately needed from each other's bodies in a frenzy. Again and again, he fucked all of her pain away.

Sy rested his forehead to Carys's and they panted in unison, their breaths slowing more and more with each heartbeat. Sy moved first, pulling out a handkerchief to clean himself, though his trousers would still be traitorously stained. He probably wouldn't care if anyone saw anyway, but Carys would fetch a maid to bring him new clothes regardless. They couldn't have people judging them for their rumpled attire.

When Carys shifted off the railing and her satin slippers touched the ground, a *ping!* sounded. Sy and Carys spotted the golden ring on the balcony at the same time. Carys stared at that ring, immobilized. Maybe it was the descent from the heady rush that made her heart so open, but the sight of that ring cracked something in her. It felt like her mother was staring up at her, just below the surface of the water, desperately reaching for Carys to hoist her above the tumultuous waves. She wondered if that's the way she looked to others around her.

No. She wouldn't become her mother. She wouldn't forever feel like she was cursed to the same fate.

Sy stooped to pick up the ring and Carys kicked it out of his reach, watching it clatter over the balcony and down onto the stable rooftop.

Sy gave her a questioning look with a laugh of surprise. It wasn't exactly out of character for Carys to be brash, if anything he seemed amused.

"It doesn't go with this dress," Carys said flatly, and Sy laughed.

Carys stared out at the open air where the ring had disappeared, hoping she could shove away the gentleness of her mother for something stronger—something that would weather the darkness that Carys seemed to always carry inside of her. Once again, she was confronted by the creeping thought that whispered into her mind: *if you keep going down this road, it will break you.*

Carys pushed that thought down deep into the dark pit that contained all of her sorrows and instead turned to Sy. "Come, my love, our guests will be expecting us."

CHAPTER FOUR

Carys had a restless sleep, which was normal after a day of heavy drinking, but what wasn't normal was the accompanying dreams. She dreamt over and over that the witches had come to notify her of her father's death. Every time she almost fell asleep she was certain she'd heard a knock on the door again, only to rise and find no one there. She found Sy slumped on the chaise lounge in the sitting area at the end of the hall—too drunk to make it to their bedroom. Carys instructed the servants to just leave him there and get to bed. Her eyes snagged on the stairwell that led toward the tower.

I should go check on him, a voice whispered in her mind. *This is the last night I'll have a chance to say goodbye.*

She tried to ignore that intuition. Not one for superstition, those pestering little voices were meant for witches, not for fae. Just because a thread of dread kept unspooling in her gut didn't mean she had to believe it.

She attempted sleep again, but the blissful rest never seemed to find her. With each nightmare, she had a rising sticky inkling that her father wouldn't be alive by dawn. Finally, she relented and decided to go see him for herself.

He'd once been her hero, the person she held in the highest

regard. Carys thought she'd done an impeccable job hiding his fall from grace within her mind. It wasn't one thing he'd done, but rather a slow degradation of his character and her growing maturity that made her realize how hollow his praise, how vicious his insults, and how meaningless the appearance of the life he displayed. She knew he mourned her mother's loss, had caught him weeping many times, but he was determined to appear like everything was all right. And she realized success to him was *appearing* successful to others, even if he was slowly dying inside, even if it made everyone around him do the same. No. He wasn't a hero to her at all anymore.

But when Carys rose from her bed for what felt like the hundredth time, she knew the decision to say a proper farewell was for the benefit of her own soul, not his.

She carried a lone candle into the gloomy room. The moonless night left her father's chamber in pitch black and she wondered if someone had blown the last candle out. Was he even still alive? She strained to hear over the pounding of her heart and heard his ragged breathing.

She tiptoed over to his bed, finding him staring vacantly at the ceiling, mouth agape and bobbing open like a fish.

"Father?" she asked, sitting gingerly beside him.

He didn't move, just kept staring.

"I'm sorry I didn't say goodbye sooner," she said, her words tight as a spring of tears spilled down her cheeks. Where this sudden burst of emotion came from, she didn't know. She cried for her father, her mother, and most of all for herself—how time had taken her father too from her and how she was so afraid of being on her own that she'd wasted her last moments with him. The resentment she harbored toward him got pushed away as she looked at him through the lens of only their happiest memories together—as if she could pick and choose the parts she needed to mourn.

"Carys."

"I'm not the person you want me to be. I'm not the person I

thought I would be either," she sniffed. She debated continuing on, but she ultimately decided if not now, then never. "And it just felt all too much, too soon. I don't want to just be Lady Hilgaard for the rest of my life, and I thought if I just ignored it, this nightmare would all end. I needed you to live so I can do more than this life. I want to be someone of my own making."

She dropped her head to the sheet that covered his chest, and his hand lifted to stroke her hair. She heard the way his chest rattled the syncopated beat of his tired heart.

"I know it doesn't make any sense. I know you're proud of the person I am even if I am not." She battled through tears to speak. "You're all the family I had left, and I wanted that pride, worthy or no. I didn't want to be all on my own."

She didn't think her father would reply, but eventually he struggled out, "You won't be alone."

"I know I have Sy, but—"

"No," he said. "Carys, listen to me," he commanded, and she knew he was rationing his words with his belabored breaths. "You have an older sister."

Her brows furrowed in confusion; at first she thought madness might have claimed him in his last moments.

"Her name is Morgan," he said. "She lives in Wynreach."

"How can that be?"

"She's a halfling," he said, and Carys gasped, her veins filling with ice. "I don't know what came over me. I-I'm sorry. Her mother must've used a witch, I think, to pull me in with a love spell or something. I never meant to hurt your mother, but I couldn't let Morgan suffer for my mistakes either."

A flicker of fear shot through her, a sudden understanding, the sunlight in her mind finally shining blindingly upon the truth. Her tears of sorrow shifted to tears of anger as she lifted her head and glared at him in his pitiful state.

"Did Mother know?" She already dreaded the answer; somewhere deep in her heart she knew.

"The day she found out," he rasped, "was the day you found her."

Her eyes welled as she pounded her fist into the mattress. Screwing her eyes shut, she pictured her mother swinging from the stable rafters. The truth was she didn't know if it was even a true memory, if she'd simply been told of what happened and her brain had conjured the image. She'd only been three years old. Each servant told her the tale of her mother's death with such inconsistency that she'd puzzled together a memory that wasn't even her own. The only truth she knew for certain: she'd been the one to find her mother.

"None of this is Morgan's fault," her father pushed, pulling her from her reeling thoughts. Bile burned up her throat. He was more concerned about this halfling than he was for her own mother? Vengeance ignited in her sternum and blossomed down her limbs. "Nor is it your fault. You should go to her, Carys, she is your family. Sy will tell you where she is."

Her plans for vengeance came to a crashing halt. Carys's whole body felt like it had been dropped off a cliff at that.

"Sy?" Her words were a hollow scratch. "He knew?"

"He's been handling sending the funds to her since I've taken ill."

"He knew all this time?" The betrayal slammed through her like a horse kick to the sternum.

"C-c-" Her father's words tripped over the first letter of her name, his breathing increasingly shaky as he reached for her. She stepped out of his grasp, standing over him, holding her candle aloft as she watched the life fade from his eyes.

CHAPTER FIVE

arys waited in the pre-dawn light of their bedroom, waiting for Sy to wake from his drunken stupor and make it down the hallway. She waited, and plotted, and stewed, every hour ticking by making her rage and heartbreak double. Like a tether finally cut loose, her mind seemed to break apart, and it was terrifying and liberating all at once. One thing she knew for certain: she was done with this gilded prison and everyone in it . . . including her Fated.

She heard the jingle of the doorhandle, the creak of the door, and waited until Sy closed their bedroom door to strike the candle to life beside her.

"Gods . . ." Sy jolted. "Carys, wh—" His words died off as he took in the expression on her face. "What happened? Is . . . is he gone?"

"He is," she said tightly, fighting to keep the angry tears from welling as she stood and balled her hands by her sides.

She needed a sword, and a dagger . . . and a knife for good measure. She needed to learn how to wield all those weapons just so she could find the best way to draw out the pain she wished to inflict on the traitor in front of her. Her sword tutor never instructed her in the art of torture—a woeful oversight on his part now.

Sy, misreading her emotions, swarmed forward, trying to wrap her up in a comforting hug.

She shoved him forcefully away and he stumbled backward. "Don't. Touch. Me."

Sy reared his head back as though struck, his eyes flaring with concern. "What happened?"

"Is there anything you want to tell me, Sy? Anything at all?" She knew it was petty to goad him, but part of her needed this. Give him one last chance to make this right, one last flicker of hope that she didn't have to be all alone. Give her a reason to not tear her entire world apart . . . but he didn't take it.

"I don't know what you're talking about," he said with a disbelieving shake of his head. So wide-eyed, and innocent, and convincingly deceptive.

Absolute fucking snake. How had she not seen it before?

"Right, then." Carys swallowed the giant rock burning down her windpipe and blinked back the burning tears. She wiggled the ruby engagement ring off her finger.

"Carys, what's going on? What are you doing?" Sy's words grew frantic as she held the heavy ring balled in her palm. "Is this . . . are you nearing your cycle?"

The question filled her with such burning fury she thought she might kill him for asking it. Yes, her cycles were the most horribly debilitating pain. Yes, the pendulum of her emotions swung wildly before she bled. But to blame her wanting to end their engagement on her body?

"I know how to help with that," Sy added with a mischievous waggle of his brows. He reached for her and she darted out of his grasp.

"You think you can fuck this away?" Carys barked.

"Can't I always?" He laughed for a moment before his brows furrowed. His sleepy drunkenness finally realizing the severity of this moment, finally taking her seriously for once. "What is this all about, then?"

"Tell me, Lord Ersan," Carys hissed. "Does the name Morgan ring any bells?"

Sy's eyes grew impossibly wide as they dropped to the ring in her hands. All at once, she saw the crashing wave of realization hit him.

"He told you."

"He told me," Carys snarled.

Sy held up his hands like he was trying to calm a skittish horse, the patronizing act so infuriating that Carys hurled the ring at him. He tried to dodge out of its way, but it collided with his cheek, leaving a satisfying cut before clattering to his feet.

"Do you know how much that cost?" He gaped down at the ring as he held his bleeding cheek and Carys bared her teeth through welling eyes. He sounded just like her father.

"I don't know who you are." Angry tears spilled down her cheeks. "The person I thought you were would've never kept this from me. Were you planning on living out our days together holding on to this lie? Always deceiving me?" She was screaming now, her words shredding her throat. "Tell me! Why did you lie to me?"

"Carys, please," Sy begged, holding up beseeching hands.

"I'm done with this," she spat. "It's over."

"Over?" He choked on the word. "It can't be over. I'm your Fated."

"You're a stranger to me!" She paced back and forth like a caged animal, knowing she needed to get out of there. "Pack your things. I'm going for a long walk and I expect you to be halfway to Arboa before I get back."

"No," he growled, taking a possessive step toward her. "I won't let you do this."

"Let me?" she replied with a laugh. "You think you have a choice now? You had a choice to tell me about my *sister* and you didn't take it." She angrily palmed her tears. "Why? Why wouldn't you tell me?"

"I . . . " As his words faltered, fury rose in Carys like a crashing wave. Instead of giving her an answer, Sy reached out and grabbed her by the back of the neck and pulled her into a burning, hot kiss.

She snarled into his mouth as his tongue plundered hers and she considered giving in, fucking him through her anger if only to feel better. But she couldn't let him win—wouldn't.

She took a menacing step toward him, the promise of violence in her eyes. "Get out of my way."

"Or what?" he asked, panicked. "Or you'll kill me? Where are you going? It's not even dawn—"

"Where I go is no longer your concern." She shoved him out of the way. He grabbed her arm as she reached for the door, and she yanked it away.

"Carys, please, *please* don't do this," he pleaded, his voice cracking.

She scrambled to unlock the door as he kept pushing it closed. "Please, he says," she growled, finally prying the door free and elbowing him in the gut. "Not sorry. Not why. Just please."

"Carys," he cried, all of his steel and resolve gone now.

"I never want to hear my name on your lips again!" she barked as she stormed down the hallway.

Sy raced after her, hands circling around her waist and hauling her back against him. She screamed and flailed, but his vice-like grip didn't budge. She swore to herself she'd never be so helpless to defend herself again. Never again would she feel weak.

"Let me go!" she wailed.

"Please, please," Sy muttered like a chant. "I can't lose you too."

All of that archery and swordsmanship failed her in the moment. She was trained in combat skills in the way of a Lady, not of a warrior, and she felt every deficiency in the way Sy so easily manhandled her.

Finally Carys's hand skimmed across Sy's belt and she felt the hilt of his ceremonial dagger there. It was an emerald-encrusted relic—one he'd never used. Still, she unsheathed the weapon and swiped at his leg. He barked out a cry as she attempted to stab his outer thigh. The odd angle of the blow didn't pierce his trouser legs, but she bet it hurt as he dropped her.

She landed on her feet, whirling around and shoving him against the wall, his dagger held flush against the skin of his throat. The blade wasn't particularly well cared for or sharpened, but she knew if she pushed hard enough it would do the trick.

"If you say another word . . ." Carys panted, her chest heaving as she gave him a look that promised she meant every single fucking word. "If you follow me. If you are here when I return, I will shove this blade straight through your fucking heart, Ersan Almah."

She shoved him away, holding his dagger out toward him as she slowly backed down the hall. He watched her, frozen, tears streaming down his cheeks, and she knew his soul was shattering into a million pieces right along with hers.

He blinked and twin tears trailed from his eyes. "Goodbye," he whispered.

And she turned and ran out into the night.

CHAPTER SIX

She took the narrow road that cut straight northward, trekking into the early morning light. Carys nicked a servant's dress off the line—a plain velvet brown—and discarded her tear-stained nightgown halfway through the gardens. As the hours wore on, Carys wondered how far she was from the border with The High Mountain Court. She'd sobbed for the first hour until she was certain she'd used every drop of moisture left in her body. Luckily she'd brought two bottles of wine with her. After drinking one empty and shattering it against the nearest tree trunk, she sobbed some more, her voice hoarse, her heart completely broken.

This pain—this fiery unearthly pain—that made her chest spasm and her limbs leaden finally ebbed in blissful numbness. And Gods, did it feel good to feel nothing but emptiness.

She kept Sy's dagger tucked into her belt, wishing she could throw it into the scrub brush but thinking better of it. Her father always forbade her from walking in these parts. He said that King Vostemur claimed red witches ran amok on the Southern Court border, and the last thing she needed was to be killed in retribution.

The bright fuchsias and marigolds of the springtime trees

faded into a singular lavender. All around her, the trees shed their purple petals until she walked upon an amethyst carpet. The scent was divine, and she decided this was where she was meant to rest. She found a moss-covered rock and perched upon it, surveying the vines beyond the violet trees that weaved above her head through the canopy like the laces of a corset.

She should turn back now. With any luck, Sy would be gone. She needed to speak to the staff, make the announcements of her father's death, and prepare the arrangements for his funeral. She should be mourning, but instead her mind was planning what finger food to pair with the funeral wine. Duty called upon her to be all the things a fae Lady was trained to be. But she didn't have the stomach for a single bit of it. She couldn't go back to fake parties and fake smiles and a fake life like the one that drove her mother to end her life. She'd never felt more close to her mother than in that moment. Both of them betrayed by their Fated. Both of them lied to by the one person who was meant to love them above all else.

She understood why her mother did it. Gods, did she understand, and she hated that understanding and resented Sy even more for it.

Her eyes drifted to the tree above her again, and to the thick vines that twined and twisted over its branches, draped like garlands, and she wondered how long it would take . . . and she imagined . . .

She didn't know how long she stared up at those noose-like vines before a voice called out, "Hello, there!"

Carys grabbed the dagger from where it lay forgotten along with the wine bottle by her feet. She held it out as she whirled toward the sound of the voice. The woman had golden hair and ocean-blue eyes that carried a weariness of a hard-lived life. Her mouth quirked into a grin as she looked at Carys's dagger as if she too knew Carys didn't know how to use it.

"You won't be needing that," she vowed. Her fingertips licked with flames the deepest shade of bronze and her eyes flared a matching color. "I'm a healer, not a fighter," she added with a laugh.

"You're a witch," Carys spat.

"I am," the witch said evenly, straightening her shoulders and flashing a lined smile. "My name's Evelyn. I was traveling southward and I sensed you were injured. I came to see—"

"Some witch you are," Carys balked. "I'm not hurt."

Evelyn's eyes crinkled as they narrowed at her. "But you are hurting, aren't you?"

Carys's bottom lip jutted out at that. She must look in a terrible state. Her eyes were probably ringed with red, her nose probably an unseemly shade of crimson.

"Something like that," she finally admitted. She sheathed the dagger through her belt again, though her shoulders remained bunched around her ears as she asked, "What is a brown witch doing in these parts?" Her eyes fell to the traveling pack leaning against a nearby tree. "Where are you off to?"

"Hilgaard Castle," the witch said. "I've been sent by Lord Berecraft of Murreneir." She hooked her finger around her witch's collar and pulled as if it had suddenly become too tight. "Sensitive topic," she added hastily. "Can't say too much. I trust I'm headed in the right direction?"

"You're headed in the right direction," Carys said with a weary sigh, the sorrow blossoming in her anew. "But I'm afraid your services won't be needed any longer. Lord Hilgaard passed this last night."

"You must be his daughter, then," Evelyn said. "The one who sent the letter." Carys bobbed her chin. "I'm sorry I was too late."

"I'm sorry you've come all this way for nothing, on foot no less."

Evelyn shrugged. "It was nice to get out of the North, however brief." She shifted her weight uncomfortably, fiddling with her hands as she asked, "So what will you do now?"

Carys glanced back up at the vines, then pinched the bridge of her nose and sighed. "I suppose become the Lady Hilgaard, take up where my father left off."

"Is that what you want?"

"What kind of a question is that?" Carys glared at the witch. "As if I have a choice."

"Don't you?" The witch cocked her head. "If I were to flee from my apothecary shop without special permission, I would be *killed*. There are people I wish I could run from, people I wish I could run *toward*, but can't. And even if this world changes, even if I were allowed, I don't know if I ever could because I was forced to make the worst sort of choices and I can never face the people I've harmed for them, only ever hiding in my apothecary and helping from the shadows. Shame owns me more than a fae Lord ever could. Can you say such things?" Carys opened her mouth to speak and closed it again as Evelyn continued. "Would you have the courage to keep going? If the castle was gone and all responsibilities to the life you lived along with it . . ."

"But it's not—"

"But it *could* be."

"What are you saying?"

"I was traveling through the south on a trip, for no other reason," Evelyn said with a confident nod, "when I stumbled past Hilgaard castle." Thunder rumbled overhead, and Evelyn looked up. "There was a storm. Lightning must've struck the building. Lord Hilgaard didn't have time to escape." Carys watched frozen as the witch unspooled a tale so perfectly designed. "The young Lady of the house decided intent not to rebuild but to travel east instead."

"East?"

"To Wynreach." Evelyn's eyes flared with magic again as she spoke as if overcome with emotions. "To find new friends, new allies, perhaps even a new family."

Carys furrowed her brow at that. What did this witch know? Maybe she was so drunk this whole thing was an illusion. Maybe she'd tripped and fell and hit her head on a rock.

But maybe this witch had a point too . . . Maybe she needed to burn down one life to start another. Maybe that thought was pounding to break free in her mind and finally this witch gave her permission to do it.

Carys stood on shaking legs, gripping tight the neck of the wine bottle in her hands.

"Thank you," she said, giving the witch a nod. "For your discretion on this matter." She fumbled for the coin purse tied to her belt, producing three golden coins.

The witch arched her golden brow, amused, but didn't protest as Carys placed the three coins in her palm. Being a witch in the Northern Court probably meant little pay, if any. Before Carys could pull back, the witch grabbed her wrist, flipped her hand over and placed two silver *druni* in her palm.

Carys stared down at the moon phases marked upon the gleaming circles. The leaving of two silver *druni* was called a "witch's goodbye." Whenever someone saw the two silver coins left on a table or dresser, they knew the witch was gone.

"Goodbye for now, Carys Hilgaard. I have a feeling I'll be seeing you again," the witch said as she gave Carys's hand a gentle squeeze and then stepped away to grab her pack. Her eyes flared bronze once more. "May your life be full of adventure and stories and peace, but most of all, may it be full of people who bring you joy."

If the witch knew how her words had stripped Carys's soul bare, she didn't show it as she offered a casual half-smile and hoisted her pack onto her shoulders. She wandered up the trail without looking back. Carys gripped the *druni* so tightly they bit into her palm, and then she turned back down the trail at a jog as thunder roiled overhead.

CHAPTER SEVEN

The sun should've been high in the sky, but a thick layer of storm clouds blotted out its golden rays. By the time Carys returned to Hilgaard castle, stumbling on drunken legs, the sky was a dark brooding gray streaked with flashes of lightning. A maid ran out, steadying her by the elbows and guiding her to sit on a garden bench just outside the front gates.

"Lady Carys, are you unwell?"

Carys wrenched her elbows away. "I am very well, Grace. Better than I've ever been," she muttered bitterly.

"You must come inside, My Lady," Grace said. "A storm's coming."

"That it is," Carys said with a smirk. She glared with bleary eyes up at the middle-aged maid. "How many staff still reside in the castle, Grace?" She'd fired so many over the last few months she had no clue how many remained.

"Only seven, My Lady," Grace said, her throat bobbing with nerves. "Are you planning to excuse more? Is it . . . is it time?"

She hated the way Grace didn't just ask if her father was dead, as if the question itself was too indelicate. Carys had already worked out a contingency plan with her staff in the event of her father's death. The members of the household had already been paid a hefty sum to keep her father's secret and had been instructed that they would find future employ at the castle in Saxbridge or in Arboa. Neelo Emberspear, despite being young in years, was the true brains behind the running of Saxbridge, and they had promised positions to everyone Carys had let go. So had Ersan, but Carys wasn't about to take him up on that offer now. Carys had planned on moving to Arboa and marrying Ersan once her father died, using Hilgaard Castle as a holiday home . . . but Grace didn't need to know of her change of plans.

"My Lady, is it time?" Grace asked again.

Carys hated the way she asked it, so timid, so fearful of Carys's power. It shouldn't be that way. Carys was still a girl in so many ways, and yet she was inheriting all of this power. And she knew for certain then that she deserved none of it. That nagging feeling that had been building and building within her finally pulled to the forefront of her mind. Staying in this life, being Lady Hilgaard, pretending she was worthy of it until time and practice made her believe she deserved every ounce . . . it would kill her.

"I'm sorry, Grace, it's time," Carys said, feigning lament. "Saxbridge will be better for you anyway. More shops and food and festivals than you'd find all the way out here. Your family is there, aren't they?" Despite Grace practically raising Carys, she couldn't seem to remember. There's wasn't a fond relationship like that of Neelo and Rish though. Carys was a job to Grace, and even though she was kind-hearted, there was no real love there.

Grace clenched a hand to her chest. "Oh, My Lady—"

"You know where the key to our coins is, yes?" Carys continued, pushing past the maid's horrified expression. Grace barely nodded. "Good. I want you to go take all of the gold within it and divvy it up amongst the seven of you."

"My Lady," Grace balked. "That's a lifetime's worth of wages."

"Take it," Carys ordered. "And anything else you can carry. You have until nightfall. When I return, you all must be gone."

Grace's face shifted from an expression of sorrow to one of fear. "No," Grace said, her voice cracking. Carys gave her a puzzled look. "Where is Lord Ersan? Why isn't he here comforting you? Did something happen—"

"Enough, Grace," Carys snapped, uncomfortable with this foreign compassion coming from her servant

"I know what you're doing," Grace continued, uncowed for once by Carys's brash temper. "I was there the day your mother . . . did it. I know what's happening."

She noted how carefully Grace said "it" as if the sting of the actual words would be the thing that did Carys in.

"Don't pretend as if you know me," Carys snarled, rising to a stand.

"You're upset right now," Grace pushed. "Perhaps we should wait until the morning—"

"Nightfall, Grace," Carys barked. "Anyone remaining will be going down with me."

Grace stumbled backward at that and fled toward the servant's quarters. Carys had contain a laugh at the sight. So much for Grace staying and fighting for her . . . a trait everyone in her life seemed to lack. Maybe she was unworthy of fighting for. It didn't matter now. She was cut loose, untethered, and she'd make the most of her demise.

Carys stormed back into the palace, determined to drink the wine cellar dry before sunset, and then she'd dance in the flames of her former life.

CHAPTER EIGHT

S omething broke open within Carys when she shattered the oil lamp in her father's room. She watched as the flames licked up the walls, eating the peeling wallpaper and consuming the room in flame. It wasn't until the flames and smoke completely obscured his lifeless body that she turned to the doorway. She leaked a trail of oil all of the way down the tower, swinging it here and there, watching as it caught fire in a scorching line behind her.

More than once she had to pat out the flames that caught her skirts alight. But she didn't feel the blistering heat, her body completely numb to it all as she discarded one oil lamp and grabbed another. Slowly and methodically she wandered through every room, farewelling her old life by setting it alight until the roar and crackle of the upper floor was deafening. When she was certain the whole place would be nothing but cinders, she traipsed out to the garden as ashes danced around her. Sitting amongst the arbor of rambling coral roses—the roses her mother had once planted long ago—she watched the flames consume her childhood home.

Something dark and twisted in her delighted in it, watching everything that bound her to this world go up in flame. But the bigger part of her mourned as if someone else had been the one to light the blaze. She watched with an equal mixture of joy and horror as the tower holding her father's body collapsed, incinerating into thick flakes of ashes. Lightning flashed overhead, illuminating the distant forest, and Carys knew within the hour a rainstorm would probably quell the inferno.

The springtime monsoons brought deluges of water, enough to make the river rise up nearly to the castle. The waterfalls would be gushing soon, the riverbeds teeming with life once more. She plucked the wine bottle—one of three she'd left for herself by the garden bench—and took another burning swig. She burped loudly and cackled, knowing no one was around for miles to hear. It felt strange and terrifying, to exist without being watched. Her every word and movement had always been dictated by the people around her—her whole life a performance. Now, with no one watching, she swung from fits of laughter to sobbing and back again. She felt rudderless and adrift and very nearly hopeless . . . but a tiny little ember still lived deep within her soul holding one singular truth: she had a sister. She needed to look this halfling Morgan in the eyes. She needed to hang on for that moment, and maybe after that, she'd have another one to reach for.

Carys teetered on the edge of drunken madness as the rainstorm descended, laughing as the cleansing water drenched her. The castle sizzled and spat as the rain battled the fire. Wood groaned, and then the stables collapsed.

A barked cry rang out through the night and Carys froze. The rain dampened the sound enough that she wondered if she'd just imagined it. Maybe it was the sounds of the fire? Listening more keenly, she heard another groan and shot to her feet. As she raced toward the stables, she lost her satin slippers in the wet earth.

A million worries raced through her mind: Had one of the staff remained? Was it a looter, who thought themselves an opportunist and got trapped? Was it someone seeking misguided refuge from the storm? Had her reckless actions just condemned someone to death?

Her toes squelched through the muck as she dashed, her hemline soaking up water all the way to her knees. She leapt over the debris, some still hissing and crackling, others just charred wood and ash. Hopping over half-burnt shutters and patches of shattered glass, she followed the strings of groans and muttered curses, pulling up the wood paneling to unearth the body below it.

When she saw who it was, she nearly dropped the paneling back down on him.

Lord Ersan of Arboa lay there in the rubble, his face twisted in pain.

Carys's first instinct was to drop to her knees and lift the smoking beam off his foot . . . her second instinct was to take his dagger and drive it straight through his heart for coming back when she told him not to. Ultimately, she decided on doing neither.

"Why did you come back here?" She shouted to be heard above the rainstorm. Trying to sound indifferent, her tone was unsure and her words slurred from two straight days of drinking many—*many*—bottles of wine.

"Ring . . ." Ersan gritted out the words through clenched teeth. He winced at the cracked wooden beam pinning down his foot, shaking over his trapped limb.

Carys let out a mirthless laugh. He wasn't here for her. Not to apologize. Not to explain himself and his secrets. Ersan was here for the expensive ring. The hideously large ruby that she'd pretended to love because every single fucking thing in her life was pretend. The ring was what he'd come back for—a dragon after his treasure. And she wondered not for the first time if she was just another piece of treasure to Ersan. He may have loved her, but he valued her like a possession too. Another prize he could brandish on his arm. A fine fae Lady for his wife. That was all she was ever meant to be—a garish shining gem to make the other fae of Okrith jealous.

No more.

Whatever became of her, however long she still had the will to exist, each second of it would be a life of her choosing. She wouldn't be pretty or dainty or poised. She would be brash and brave and fearsome.

She took out the two silver *druni* and dropped them onto his writhing body with a *plink, plink.*

"If you won't leave the ruins of our life together like I asked of you, then I will, Ersan," she said. Ersan winced again, and this time she thought it wasn't from the pain of his crushed foot.

"Carys!" he called out as she turned back to her garden bench. He screamed for her over and over as she plodded her way barefoot through the muck. Picking up her remaining bottle of wine, she trudged onward through the pouring rain and turned down the trail eastward. It would take her all of the night and most of the next day to reach Westdale and the boat that could ferry her across to Wynreach. Then she'd face this Morgan and decide if she could survive without the Fated she'd left behind.

CHAPTER NINE

She wandered aimlessly through the woods, bereft. No shawl, no pack, nothing to her name but the absurd gown she was wearing, the emerald dagger through her belt, and the now empty bottle of wine still in her grip. She had no money, no change of clothes. Gods, she didn't even have any fucking shoes.

Carys knew she probably should've thought it through more, probably should've packed her belongings and arranged a carriage before setting the house alight. But none of the past two days made any sense. Her father was gone, her Fated betrayed her, so she could be excused for her poorly calculated burst of fiery rage.

The darkest parts of her hoped the castle had crumbled atop Ersan. But deep in her soul she knew he would be fine if only to torture her the rest of her life. It probably would've been easier if he'd died amongst the rubble. Every few steps she debated turning back and had to force herself to keep going. She hated the waves of guilt and desire to return to him, even after everything he'd done. Curse this Fated bond and the magic that bound her to him. Why couldn't she sever this cord between them? Why hadn't it incinerated along with everything else?

Ersan would live even with a shattered foot—the stables too far to do him damage from any falling debris and the rainstorm too thorough to reignite the flames. Carys wondered if he lay there still, trapped and waiting for aid. She wondered if he was in a terrible amount of pain. And she wondered if it amounted to anything close to the pain she felt within herself.

Soon news of the fire would spread across Okrith. Her ex-servants would arrive in Saxbridge and send people back to scavenge the wreckage . . . if the Arboan bandits didn't get to it first. Either way, Ersan would be found and brought to witch healers. He'd be fine, even if Carys never would be again.

Her whole body trembled as she walked, her feet cut open and bleeding. Despite the springtime heat of the midday sun, she felt like she'd bathed in ice water. It was probably the come down after the shock, the bravado the wine brought her starting to wear off. She kept moving, battling for each step, hoping at every turn the tavern at Westdale would appear.

She heard the sound of horses' hooves clomping through the wet earth before she spotted them. It wasn't until she reached the crossroads that the two riders were revealed. Carys's shoulders drooped in relief. She knew the two of them—twins from the Eastern Court and good friends of its crown prince. Twin Eagles, many called them; golden-eyed and auburn-haired, they took in Carys's sorry state.

Talhan let out a low whistle. "Carys Hilgaard, what a pleasant surprise." He said the word "pleasant" like a question. "Are you traveling on your own? Had a big night?" he asked with a waggle of his eyebrows. Carys just blinked back at him, his words taking longer than normal to process.

"Where's that Lord who's always attached to you?" Briata asked with a wry grin. "You two couldn't get your tongues out of each other's mouths long enough to even drink at my cousin's wedding."

"I am no longer together with Lord Ersan." Carys was proud

of how steady the words came out of her mouth despite her eyes welling.

"Wh—" Talhan started, but his twin shot him a look as if to say, "Cut it out."

"I left him last night," Carys croaked, wrinkling her nose in an attempt to stymy the tears.

Briata scanned Carys from her matted hair to the mud-stained hem of her dress. "And all you brought with you was a dagger and a bottle of wine?" Briata's smirk pulled her lips up at the corners. She looked at her twin and murmured, "I think I love her."

"Where are you headed?" Talhan asked, ignoring his sister.

"Wynreach," Carys replied. She kept her gaze on the ground, sniffing and wiping her eyes, not wanting to see any pity in their gazes.

"Well, lucky for you, we are headed there ourselves," Briata said. "Why don't you accompany us? We'll take you as far as Wynreach, then we leave for our next harebrained mission on behalf of His Royal pain in my ass, King Norwood."

Carys's ears perked up at that. A soldier in an army. She imagined it for a moment. No one would question her if she was a soldier for a crown prince, even the Bastard Prince Hale. She sized the twins up—their muscled figures, the litany of weapons strapped to them, the confidence with which they moved through space. They probably never feared anything. No one with any common sense would ever pick a fight with either of them. Their steadiness and strength held a mirror up to Carys in a way that made envy bloom in her gut. Everything felt so uncertain, but this golden-eyed pair in the middle of the jungle, they seemed certain.

"How is one selected for the crown prince's army?" Carys asked. "Is it by the King's council or does His Highness select them himself?"

"Selected?" Talhan guffawed. "More like condemned."

"Tal and I volunteered," Briata offered. "But every other poor soul was sent to us. The majority are humans. A few witches without enough magic to find other lines of work. Criminals mostly."

"Criminals?"

"They're given a choice: the gallows or five years in Hale's retinue."

Carys's brow crinkled. "Surely five years of work is the better option?"

Talhan winced and tipped his head side to side as if weighing his answer. "The life expectancy isn't particularly high in Hale's crew."

"Okay," Carys replied.

"Okay?" the twins echoed in unison.

Carys folded her wet arms across her puffed-out chest. "I'd like to join."

"Well, fuck me," Briata said. "Not literally. *Although* . . ."

"She's just broken up with her Fated and already you're trying to hit on her?" Talhan muttered.

"I'm not trying anything," Briata countered. "It's not my fault if I'm just naturally very charming."

Talhan snorted. "Come on." He dismounted and offered his horse's reins out to Carys. "My legs are tighter than an archer's bowstring." He rubbed his thighs and shook out each leg. "I much prefer trekking. I'll lead the horses, you ride."

"Gives us some time to dissuade you from whatever fallacious sights you've set on joining our crew," Briata added pointedly.

When Carys took the offered reins, her hands were so shaky she could barely hold them aloft. Talhan stepped up to her and held his hands hovering around her waist. "May I?" he asked softly. When Carys nodded, he grabbed her gently around the waist and lifted her onto his horse.

"Thank you," she said so quietly the words barely came out.

"There," Talhan said, looking over his shoulder at his twin. "How about that for chivalry?"

Briata snorted. "In a competition of charms, I'd still win."

"Care to put a wager on that?"

Carys couldn't help but chuckle as she wiped away her tears. Briata's horse shifted closer, and she patted Carys's leg.

"It's going to be okay, you know?" Briata said, and for the briefest beautiful second, Carys believed her.

CHAPTER TEN

They arrived at Westdale tavern within the hour, Talhan's legs eating up the distance with such speed it rivaled the horses. The rest of the day went by in a hollow blur. When they arrived at the tavern, the twins handled everything, whisking Carys off to the bath houses while a tavern worker procured her a change of clothes. Carys let them guide her through the motions of normalcy, even though she barely spoke to them in response. Her mind seemed so separate from her body, her thoughts living outside of herself now. The Twin Eagles had no problem carrying on a conversation without her though.

That night, the Eagles set up permanent residence in the bar. Carys feigned exhaustion and they bid her goodnight, but she knew sleep would be too far from her reach. The room was too small, the noises from the bar too loud, and whenever she stepped over the threshold of her bedchamber, her heart began galloping inside her ribcage. Her body wasn't fit for sleep.

Instead of torturing herself to a restless night, she slipped out the back door of the tavern and walked down to the shores of the Crushwold River. She needed the cool water on her feet to calm her racing heart. The bite of the chilly water made gooseflesh ripple up her calves, but it did the trick.

Of course, when her heart slowed, the emotions welled again.

She stared up at the waning silver moon, finding she didn't have the will to fight the rising storm within her. Finally she permitted herself the tears that she'd been holding in all day. They silently slid down her cheeks as everything flooded through her like a crashing wave. Her father was dead. Her Fated would never be hers again. *Nothing* felt real. If she suddenly gasped awake and the day started anew she wouldn't even question it. How desperately she wished the last three months had all been a long, elaborate nightmare. When would she wake from this torment?

And somehow through the misery, she managed to get to Westdale and then volunteered to be a soldier in the Eastern prince's army? Everything was crumbling down around her. What had she done?

Her cries were cut short when she heard the snap of a twig behind her. A body walked up beside hers—Briata. Hands in pockets, the Eagle stared up to the moon alongside her for several breaths before she finally reached over and put a comforting hand on Carys's shoulder.

"Whatever he did must've been pretty awful," Briata finally said. "I wish I could stab him for you. I still can if you'd like?"

Carys huffed a laugh at the Eagle's twisted version of comfort. "I don't want to talk about him, Briata."

"My friends call me Bri," she said simply. "You should call me Bri."

Carys sniffed again at that little act of kindness. "Bri," she croaked. "I don't think you stabbing Ersan would make me feel any better."

"Of course it would." Bri clapped her on the shoulder and then moved to pull the emerald dagger from Carys's waistband. "But it would feel even better if *you* stabbed him yourself. Do you even know how to use this thing?" she asked, twirling the blade around and inspecting the emerald-studded hilt.

Carys bristled. "I've been trained."

"By who?" Bri let out a derisive laugh. "Let me guess. You were trained by someone who taught you how to bow politely at the end of every perfectly choreographed scuffle? Some pompous old Lord who never once saw combat but calls himself a fighting instructor?"

Carys folded her arms and popped her hip to the side. "Lord Faridell is very apt—"

"Ah, they got you Faridell, eh?" Bri snickered. "Lord Faridell is one strained bowel movement away from passing away into the afterlife." She flipped the hilt of the dagger over and handed it back to Carys. "Come on, land a strike. You can delight me with the tales of your tribulations while we spar."

"It's the middle of the night," Carys pointed out, waving to the moon.

"And that stops us training *because*?" Bri circled her hand in a wheeling motion, waiting for Carys to reply.

Carys pursed her lips. "It's dark. I . . . I might hurt you."

Before Carys could even get the whole sentence out, Bri doubled over with laughter. Clutching her stomach, she cackled as if Carys had just told the world's greatest joke. She pinched her side and swiped at her eyes as Carys scowled back at her.

"I'm sorry," Bri wheezed. "It's just too good."

Carys gripped the dagger harder until her knuckles turned white. "It's not that funny."

"It is." Bri fanned herself, sucking in deep breaths of air. "For so many reasons, not the least because that blade is as blunted as a butter knife and even with the strength of ten soldiers you wouldn't be able to pierce it through my leathers."

"It might still bruise though."

"I like bruises," Bri said with a mischievous wink. "I think you'll come to like them too."

Bri flapped her hand forward, beckoning Carys to attack.

Carys debated indulging the Golden Eagle for a brief moment before ultimately giving in and launching forward. She moved her blade in the proper formations just as she'd been instructed. Within a single breath, Bri had easily grabbed the dagger out of her grip and booted her to the side, making Carys topple over and land on all fours.

Carys snarled from her hands and knees as Bri flipped the dagger around and offered her the hilt.

"Again," Bri commanded.

Scowling, Carys rose and took the dagger, launching into an attack with twice the speed. She managed to keep Bri's reaching hands at bay for a few moments but was too focused on their upper bodies to notice when Bri's boot hooked her ankle. She fell flat on her back and the air whooshed out of her lungs.

Bri offered her hand down to Carys. "Again."

"I think you've made your point," Carys snapped, dusting the leaves and dust off of her freshly acquired clothes.

"Oh, I would disagree entirely." Bri chuckled as she hoisted Carys back to her feet. "Now, let's go again and you can tell me about your shitty excuse of a Fated."

The question surprised Carys, halfway to her first strike. The memory of Ersan lit a new fire in her—the feeling of hopelessness turning into something feral. How dare he do this to her? How dare he lie. How dare he make her the fool who trusted him. Baring her teeth, she launched herself at Bri.

"Oh-ho!" Bri exclaimed delightedly as Carys attacked with a newfound ferocity. "So the Lady has claws after all."

Carys finally found an opening and struck, landing a punch to Bri's jaw and striking her leathers just below the rib with her dagger. Bri was entirely unfazed, only reacting with laughter. Bri's expression was one of mischievous glee as if Carys's attack was the greatest thing that'd ever happened to her. Carys had the distinct impression that Bri was letting her land these blows, but still, it felt great to exhaust some of that fury in her.

Finally, Bri grabbed Carys by the wrist and easily maneuvered her around so that she had Carys's back pinned against her front, her muscled arms wrapped around Carys in a tight hug.

"You're a warrior, Carys Hilgaard," Bri said, both of their chests rising and falling in unison. "She's there under all the pleasantries, and I'm determined to bring her to the surface."

She released Carys and Carys stepped away, doubling over. She dropped her hands to her knees and drew in deep breaths. "I don't ever want to feel helpless again," Carys said between her sharp breaths.

"I don't know if I can promise that," Bri hedged. "But I can promise to help you be the strongest you can be. If you decide to come with us, we're going to rise with the dawn every day until you feel as powerful as you are." Carys's eyes misted again and Bri shoved her shoulder. "Come on, you can cry while we go again."

"Wait," Carys said, reaching back and quickly weaving her hair into a long braid. "There." She brushed the braid over her shoulder and it swished like a lion's tail at the small of her back. "Ready."

Bri and Carys spent another two hours sparring. Carys told Bri about everything: Morgan, her father, Ersan, her mother, the choices she'd been considering making.

And to her surprise, Bri shared much of her own sordid family history too. Bri's mother sounded like the most punchable person Carys had ever heard of, her father not that much better either. She didn't know that Bri had such a painful past, but it was comforting in some ways too. Bri was this strong, confident warrior. She'd found a way out from under all that pain. Carys was determined that she would do the same.

The Eagle looked like she could go for another two hours when she said, "That's enough for tonight."

Carys wanted to collapse onto the ground right there.

"Thank you for this," Carys said sheepishly as she caught her breath. "I feel . . ." What did she feel? Better? That wasn't the right word. Stronger? Perhaps a little. Whatever this training session was meant to be, it was a beautiful reprieve from all the pain she'd been feeling. At some point her mind could only focus on Bri's flying fists and her attempts to control her breathing.

As they turned back toward the tavern, Bri said, "You're going to stick around." She said it with such a determined nod as if it was already decided for her.

"You sound very certain," Carys said.

"I am." Bri flashed her brilliant, wide smile. "And we're going to train every day, rain, hail or no, until you're as certain as I am."

CHAPTER ELEVEN

The Eagles walked on either side of Carys as they wove through the streets of Wynreach. They moved shoulder to shoulder in silent solidarity with her until the roads became so narrow they had to walk single file. When they reached the last street and turned down the alleyway that the fishmonger had directed them toward, Carys paused.

Tal patted her on the back and Carys cleared her throat, shifting uncomfortably. Down this road, the eighth door on the right, was Morgan's home.

"Do you want us to come?" Bri asked.

Carys shook her head. "No. I can do this."

"Yes, you can." Talhan grabbed both of her shoulders and shook her like she was a boxer about to enter the ring.

She chuckled and his smile widened with the sound. She couldn't understand it really. She'd been friendly with these two most of her life, but it had never been like this. Never truly friends. She hadn't known anything about their pasts or their true selves until the night before. She couldn't understand why they would be willing to do all of this for her when she'd done nothing to deserve it. It felt wrong to need these people, to need anyone. She wanted to finally be independent of it all. Not Lord

Hilgaard's daughter, not Lord Almah's Fated, not someone who leaned on everyone around them, just Carys.

"We're going to grab some food down at the markets," Bri offered. "We'll probably eat at the moon fountain in the witching quarter if you want to catch us up."

If things go horribly wrong and your interaction with your sister only lasts two minutes, sounded more like what she wanted to say.

Carys swallowed the lump in her throat. "Okay."

She bobbed her head but kept her eyes fixed on the door eight down. She pressed her lips together and took a step forward, then another, coaching her feet to move. The town houses were packed together in the human quarter. Lines of washing waved high overhead and the streets were filled with the lingering smell of the fish markets, but each stoop was covered in brightly colored pots of flowers, each door beautifully painted and intricately carved. She counted her way down. And then counted again just to make sure.

The Eagles had already disappeared and she was grateful no one watched her hesitant pacing outside the door. She took a deep, slow breath. Then another. And on the third she walked up the steps and in one smooth movement rapped on the door.

She worried her lip as she waited, part of her wanting to dart down the alley before the door opened. Maybe they weren't even home. Her heart thundered in her chest, pounding against her sternum as the lock of the door clicked.

When the door opened, a beautiful woman stood on the other side. She had warm blond hair and sapphire-blue eyes, a striking resemblance to Carys in her mouth and nose. There was no point in asking if she was Morgan, the resemblance to her and her father so striking. And then there were her ears. Morgan's ears were tapered to nearly a point but then rounded at the top.

Morgan's face was wary as she assessed Carys, her expression slowly morphing from scrutiny to surprise and then something like disbelief.

"Hi," Carys said, fumbling to find her words. She anxiously clasped her hands in front of her. "I'm—"

"Carys," Morgan said, placing a hand on her stomach. "I know." Her eyes dropped to the emerald dagger sheathed on Carys's hip. "Are you here to get rid of the Lord Hilgaard's halfling, Carys?"

Carys's eyes dropped to the slight swell in her belly and held. She was pregnant? Her sister was going to have a child? She was going to be an aunt? Something about the sight overwhelmed her.

"I'm not here to hurt you." Her eyes welled until her sister was blurry. Morgan seemed to believe her as her eyes began to mist too. "I didn't know you existed until two days ago. My father—our father," she quickly remedied, "he told me on his deathbed about you, and . . ." She fumbled over her words as they came out of her in a violent rush. "I would've come if I had known." The tears streamed faster. "I wished my whole life that there was more than just me and him, that I had a big family, and I—"

Her words were cut off when Morgan shot forward and pulled her into a fierce hug. Carys's arms wrapped around her sister's warm body and held her just as tightly. She dropped her face into Morgan's shoulder and sobbed as her sister did the same.

"I'm here," Morgan said. "I'm here now."

Carys sobbed harder, not knowing how her sister somehow understood her jumbled thoughts. Morgan held on to her with all of the motherly care Carys had never known, and even though they'd only just met a heartbeat ago, something about this moment felt inevitable, not like greeting a stranger but rather a homecoming. Carys felt loved by her, and she loved Morgan in return.

The world was still coming undone all around her, but this moment, this embrace was like a salve to her soul. It was like finding a lost memory, a lost piece of herself, one that suddenly and fiercely fit within her life, and she knew there was no going back and there was no letting go. She was determined then that she'd find a way to piece together the family she'd always longed for. That maybe one day all this dark emptiness within her would one day fill with light.

I hope you enjoyed Carys's story! Carys and Sy's journey continues in The Amethyst Kingdom! If you enjoyed The Witch's Goodbye, please consider leaving a review, sharing on social media, or telling a friend! -A.K. xx

PATREON

Join A. K. Mulford's Patreon to receive ARCs, book mail, access to the Mountaineers discord server, spicy artwork, and brand new novellas!

ACKNOWLEDGMENTS

Thank you to all of my amazing patrons for making this novella possible! Your support means so much to me!

A very special thank you to my fae, royal, and goddess patrons: Audrey, Jaime, Kristie, Lauren, Linda, Marissa, Alyssa, Amy, Ciara, Crystal, Drea, Emily, Hannah, Kelly, Katie, Mandy, Latham, Sarah, Virginia, Leigh, Felicia, Mariah, Patricia, Stacy, Jessica, JeNaya, and Lauren.

Thank you to Holly Dunn for the gorgeous design of the cover and the new map.

Thank you to K. Elle Morrison for the interior formatting and designs.

Thank you to Norma Gambini from Normas Nook Proofreading for all of your support and amazing proofreading skills.

Thank you to the amazing Kate for formatting the paperbacks of these novellas and running the A.K. merch shop!

Thank you to Sara Kingsley from Adore Editing!

ABOUT THE AUTHOR

A.K. Mulford is a bestselling fantasy author and former wildlife biologist who swapped rehabilitating monkeys for writing novels.

She/they are inspired to create diverse stories that transport readers to new realms, making them fall in love with fantasy for the first time, or, all over again.

She now lives in Australia with her husband and two young human primates, creating lovable fantasy characters and making ridiculous Tiktok videos.

www.akmulford.com

ALSO BY AK MULFORD

The Okrith Novellas
The Witch of Crimson Arrows
The Witch Apothecary
The Witchslayer
The Witching Trail
The Witch's Goodbye

The Five Crowns Of Okrith Series
The High Mountain Court
The Witches' Blade
The Rogue Crown
The Evergreen Heir
The Amethyst Kingdom

The Golden Court Series
A River of Golden Bones
A Sky of Emerald Stars